WELCOM_

I SPY
HALLOWEEN

GOOD LOCK!

I SPY WITH MY LITTLE EYE , SOMETHING BEGINNING WITH ...

LET'S COLOR THE ANSWER

A IS FOR ANGEL

I SPY WITH MY LITTLE EYE , SOMETHING BEGINNING WITH ...

LET'S COLOR THE ANSWER

B IS FOR BROOMSTICK

I SPY WITH MY LITTLE EYE , SOMETHING BEGINNING WITH ...

LET'S COLOR THE ANSWER

COBWEB

I SPY WITH MY LITTLE EYE , SOMETHING BEGINNING WITH ...

I SPY WITH MY LITTLE EYE, SOMETHING BEGINNING WITH ...

LET'S COLOR THE ANSWER

EYEBALLS

I SPY WITH MY LITTLE EYE , SOMETHING BEGINNING WITH ...

LET'S COLOR THE ANSWER

FANGS

BE A R

I SPY WITH MY LITTLE EYE , SOMETHING BEGINNING WITH ...

LET'S COLOR THE ANSWER

I SPY WITH MY LITTLE EYE, SOMETHING BEGINNING WITH ...

LET'S COLOR THE ANSWER

I SPY WITH MY LITTLE EYE , SOMETHING BEGINNING WITH ...

LET'S COLOR THE ANSWER

I

IMP

I SPY WITH MY LITTLE EYE , SOMETHING BEGINNING WITH ...

LET'S COLOR THE ANSWER

B

J

JACK-O'-LANTERN

I SPY WITH MY LITTLE EYE, SOMETHING BEGINNING WITH ...

LET'S COLOR THE ANSWER

I SPY WITH MY LITTLE EYE, SOMETHING BEGINNING WITH ...

LET'S COLOR THE ANSWER

LANTERN

I SPY WITH MY LITTLE EYE , SOMETHING BEGINNING WITH ...

MAGIC WAND

I SPY WITH MY LITTLE EYE , SOMETHING BEGINNING WITH ...

LET'S COLOR THE ANSWER

I SPY WITH MY LITTLE EYE , SOMETHING BEGINNING WITH ...

LET'S COLOR THE ANSWER

I SPY WITH MY LITTLE EYE , SOMETHING BEGINNING WITH ...

LET'S COLOR THE ANSWER

PUMPKIN

I SPY WITH MY LITTLE EYE , SOMETHING BEGINNING WITH ...

LET'S COLOR THE ANSWER

QUEEN

I SPY WITH MY LITTLE EYE , SOMETHING BEGINNING WITH ...

LET'S COLOR THE ANSWER

R

ROBOT

I SPY WITH MY LITTLE EYE , SOMETHING BEGINNING WITH ...

SKULL

I SPY WITH MY LITTLE EYE , SOMETHING BEGINNING WITH ...

I SPY WITH MY LITTLE EYE , SOMETHING BEGINNING WITH ...

LET'S COLOR THE ANSWER

I SPY WITH MY LITTLE EYE , SOMETHING BEGINNING WITH ...

LET'S COLOR THE ANSWER

VAMPIRE

I SPY WITH MY LITTLE EYE , SOMETHING BEGINNING WITH ...

LET'S COLOR THE ANSWER

I SPY WITH MY LITTLE EYE , SOMETHING BEGINNING WITH ...

LET'S COLOR THE ANSWER

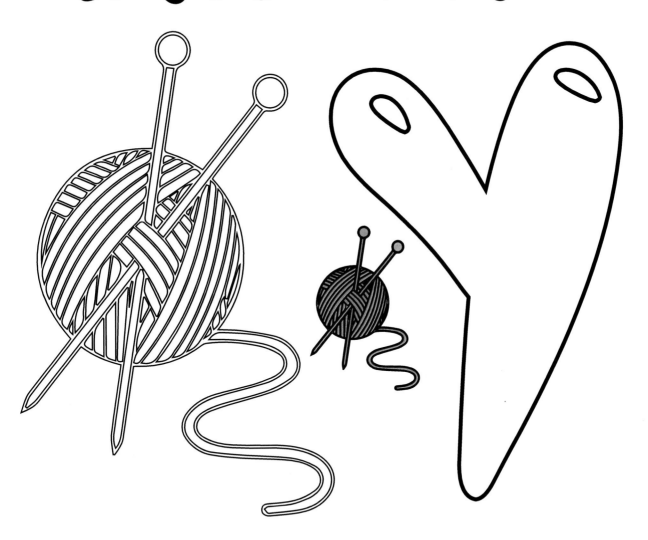

I SPY WITH MY LITTLE EYE , SOMETHING BEGINNING WITH ...

LET'S COLOR THE ANSWER

ZOMBIE

HALLOWEEN

CERTIFICATION OF COMPLETION

This Certificate is Presented to

DATE ....

HALLOWEEN

Made in the USA
Middletown, DE
08 October 2020